A FAMIL CHRIS'1

SPINSTER MAIL-ORDER BRIDES

(BOOK 5)

By

Cheryl Wright

Contents:

A Family for Christmas

(Spinster Mail Order Romance – Book Five)

Copyright ©2019 by Cheryl Wright

Cover Artist: Black Widow Books\

https://www.facebook.com/blackwidowbooks/

Thanks

Thanks to my very dear friends (and authors), Margaret Tanner and Susan Horsnell for their enduring encouragement.

Thanks also to Alan, my husband of over 44 years, who has been a relentless supporter of my writing for many years.

And last, but by no means least, I must thank all my wonderful readers who encourage me to continue writing these stories. It is such a joy to me, knowing so many of you enjoy reading my stories. I love writing them as much as you love reading them.

About the Author

Multi-published, best selling and award-winning author, Cheryl Wright, former secretary, debt collector, account manager, writing coach, and shopping tour hostess, loves reading.

She writes both contemporary and historical western romance, as well as contemporary romance and romantic suspense.

She lives in Melbourne, Australia, and is married with two adult children and has six grandchildren.

When she's not writing, she can be found in her craft room making greeting cards.

Check out Cheryl's Amazon page - https://www.amazon.com/author/cherylwright for a full list of her other books.

Other Links:

http://cheryl-wright.com

https://www.facebook.com/cherylwrightauthor

Join my newsletter here - http://cheryl-wright.com/newsletter.htm

Chapter One

Magdalena Roth helped her sister to pack.

Elizabeth and William would only be gone for a matter of days, which meant she got to spend some quality time with her little niece.

"I, I sent away to be a mail order bride," Magdalena blurted out.

Elizabeth spun around to face her. "You've what? Oh, Magdalena, what have you done?"

She bit her bottom lip. "Things are looking pretty grim for me in the marriage stakes. No one wants a spinster for a wife."

It was true, and she knew it. If she didn't do something now, it would never happen, and she'd be stuck living with her sister and her husband for the rest of her life.

"What am I going to do without you to look after Annie?"

She turned away to ensure her sister didn't see the disappointment on her face. Didn't she even care that Magdalena was to marry a complete stranger? "I leave the day after you get back. Mr Carruthers has agreed that I should visit regularly. I shall miss you all terribly otherwise."

Elizabeth nodded.

Was it true? Did Elizabeth really only care about her babysitting capabilities and nothing else? She'd always felt close to her sister – they were only a year apart in age, but now she wondered how close her sister felt to her. Or was she just a convenience since she'd lost her job?

"I'm sorry," Elizabeth said, nudging toward her sister. "I didn't mean it like that. Of course I'm happy for you." She reached out and the sisters hugged.

"I know," Magdalena said quietly. "And I'm sorry to leave you in a predicament." She stared into her sister's face.

What was she thinking?

"We'll work it out. Don't you worry about it."

"Promise?"

Elizabeth hugged her again. "Promise. I hope you'll be very happy."

Annie squawked – she wanted out of her crib. At eight months old, she was still very dependent on others, but was already developing a personality of her own.

"I'll get her – you finish packing," Magdalena said.

Elizabeth nodded.

When she and William had married, Elizabeth was already in the family way, and there was no chance to have a honeymoon. Now the baby was old enough to be away from her mother, Magdalena had offered to take care of her while they were away on their trip.

She'd happily agreed at the time, but now had reservations. Annie had recently been weaned off her mother's milk and was now eating solids, but only certain foods. It was rather fiddly, but Magdalena would go that extra mile for her little niece.

Elizabeth had worked hard to earn her nurse's certificate. It wouldn't be fair to not use it, she'd told her younger sister, and in some ways Magdalena agreed, but she wanted to pursue a life of her own.

In the end they'd decided that Elizabeth would work the late shift at the hospital, and Magdalena would take up a teaching job.

It worked out for both of them. Elizabeth got to continue with a job she loved without having to pay for a nanny. In return, Magdalena got to spend far more time with her niece than she would otherwise.

All that changed a week ago when the school board told her they were handing her teaching position to a man, for no other reason than he was male and she was not. It broke her heart.

She missed the children incredibly, even after just one week. They had been her life, her reason for getting up each day. Until something else turned up, she looked after Annie in return for board and lodgings.

When they returned from their trip, Elizabeth would return to working the day shift. What they would do now, without Magdalena there, she didn't know. Surely they'd sort something out. She tried not to think too far ahead. More than anything, it was going to be heartbreaking leaving her niece. She hoped Mr Carruthers was a decent man.

Jacob Carruthers paced the floor of his office.

With less than a week to go before his bride arrived, he was having second thoughts. He had given in to pressure that he should be married by now. Of course the unspoken caveat was he should have little heirs running around.

As Banker of Great Falls, he had an image to uphold, and this particular image had been foisted on him by his older sister, the mother of five children.

He ran his fingers through his thinning hair. At least that's what he thought. His sister Jennifer told him it was all in his imagination.

It was alright for her – she lived out of town on a huge ranch with her husband Charles. There was plenty of room for his nieces and nephews to run around.

Although his house was big, far larger than was necessary for a single man of thirty-four, he wasn't sure it was suitable for five children. Heaven forbid he ever had that many brats running around.

He wasn't even certain he wanted a wife, let alone a child.

He was staring out the window, looking across the ranges when his secretary entered the office.

"Coffee," she said, placing the mug on his desk.

He turned to face her. "I think I've messed up, Abigail," he said quietly.

Her eyebrows shot up. "What do you mean?" She'd been his secretary for over a decade, and had doubled as his confidante on the rare occasion.

He went around to the other side of his desk and sank down into the chair. "I finally gave into my sister's pressure and applied for a mail order bride." He lifted the mug and took a sip, reaching for the cookies she'd also placed on his desk.

"I can now see that was a mistake."

Abigail smiled. "That's an easy fix. Write back and cancel."

He took a huge gulp of the coffee. "If it was only that easy. She's due here at the end of the week. It's far too late to back out."

"Oh."

Oh indeed. Miss Magdalena Roth would arrive on Friday, and there was no turning back.

Magdalena leaned over the crib and stared at the sleeping baby.

11

She'd hoped to have a baby of her own one day. Still single at twenty-eight, she now doubted that would ever happen.

She loved to babysit for her sister Elizabeth. She adored little Annie, and would do anything for her.

William Harcourt was not her choice of husband for her sister, he'd been a scoundrel for as long as she could remember. And he'd got her pregnant before their marriage.

Despite all that, Elizabeth was head over heels in love with him, more's the pity.

The best thing to come out of that marriage was Annie.

They would be back tomorrow, and knowing this was their last night together for some time, Magdalena wanted to pick up the precious angel and hug her tight. But the baby was sleeping peacefully, and there was no way her aunt would disturb her.

At least she'd had Annie to herself for a whole seven days. She envied her sister the chance of a lifetime – a riverboat cruise. How exciting that must be!

Magdalena left the room quietly, heading for the kitchen. A hot cocoa would warm her up, and help her sleep. In two days she'd leave for Great

Falls, Montana, and was experiencing last minute nerves.

She never dreamed she would accept an offer as a mail order bride, but at her age, there was little choice, so that's exactly what she'd done.

It was only a few days travel on the train, so it wasn't like she'd never see her sister or niece again.

She sipped the cocoa as she sat in front of a roaring fire reading a few more pages of her book. She awoke from a deep sleep to urgent pounding on the front door.

The noise startled the baby.

Magdalena stumbled from the chair still in a half asleep stupor, torn between answering the door and picking up the crying baby.

In the end she ran to the crib and picked Annie up, comforting her as she ran to the door. It was pitch black outside – who could be calling at this ungodly hour?

"Who is it?" she yelled through the door.

"Police, Miss Roth."

She ran to the sitting room and peeked through the curtains. Two uniformed police stood on the door step. Dread filled her.

One of the officers stepped forward when she opened the door. "Miss Roth? Miss Magdalena Roth?"

She pulled Annie a little closer, her heart beating so quickly, to the point she felt faint.

"Yes, that's me."

"Might we come in, Miss Roth?" They didn't wait for an answer, instead pushed their way in, indicating for her to sit. Magdalena was feeling weak, and was grateful for the support.

"There's been an accident, Miss Roth." The first officer pulled his hat off his head, and the second one followed suit.

She gasped. "An accident? My sister, Elizabeth, she's alright isn't she?"

It was hard to breathe, and she had to force herself to take deep breaths.

"I'm afraid not, Miss Roth. The riverboat sank, killing all the passengers and crew. Both Mr and Mrs Harcourt were among them."

Dead? Elizabeth?

Magdalena fought back a sob. "What about Annie?"

The two police looked at each other. "Annie?"

"The baby," she said, cradling her dear niece. She'd never cared much for William, and shuddered at her sister's choice of husband, but that didn't mean she wasn't sorry for him. "I'm supposed to leave town in two days. I'm getting married in Great Falls," she said quietly.

She had no intention of telling them she was to be a mail order bride. Besides, her brain was full of fog right now. No doubt it was the shock of the situation.

"Are there any other relatives?"

She looked down into the innocent face of her niece and stifled a sob. "I'm the only one. But I can't..." She hugged Annie tight. "How can I..." she swallowed hard.

She stood for a moment in her confusion, then sat again. "I have no choice, do I? I'll have to take Annie with me."

The officers stood looking down at her. "I'm terribly sorry, Miss Roth," the most senior one said.

A thought suddenly popped into her head. "What about the funeral?" Did that mean she had to delay her wedding? She couldn't think right now.

"No bodies were recovered, so there won't be a funeral. You're free to leave whenever you're ready."

This was more than Magdalena could comprehend right now. She knew the moment the baby had fallen asleep again as she sagged against her shoulder.

"I'll just put her down," she said softly. As she lay Annie down in her crib, she mourned for the parents her niece would never know.

What was she to do? Jacob Carruthers had not agreed to marrying a spinster with a babe in arms. Far from it.

She risked arriving in Great Falls, only to be turned away again. But she had no choice. Now that William and Elizabeth were gone, she was homeless. The house came with William's job, and the change of circumstances meant she'd be expected to leave within the week.

Moving as gently as she could, she pulled the covers up around Annie's shoulders. The closer it got to Christmas, the colder the weather. She stood staring at the child for long moments, and then remember the constabulary waiting in the sitting room.

No doubt they were enjoying the warmth of the fire.

They were standing close to the fire when she returned. "They were to return this afternoon," she said, fighting the emotion in her voice. "And I was to leave tomorrow. Is there anything I have to do before I leave?"

"You're free to leave with the baby whenever you are ready. Goodnight Miss Roth, and Godspeed to you both."

Magdalena closed the door behind them, then sank down into the sofa close to the fire. She felt chilled all over despite the heat it produced. She shook her head trying to shake the impending doom away.

The tears that had threatened to fall when she heard the news now fell in cascades. Putting her head to her hands, Magdalena thought about her sister fighting, drowning in the murky waters of the Bighorn River. Elizabeth had never been a strong swimmer, but perhaps she may not have survived even if she was.

Her heart lurched.

She quietly checked on Annie who was sleeping soundly, then made her way to her bedroom. She'd commenced packing over the past days, the trunk already half-full of clothes. Now she had much more to do, including organizing for the baby's belongings to fit in the same trunk.

She opened her carpetbag and threw in some essentials they might need on the long rail trip, and mentally organized the costs along the way.

She opened her pocketbook. It was awfully empty, and she wasn't sure it would be enough. Then she remembered her sister had a cookie jar in the kitchen where she kept money for an emergency.

Magdalena stood at the kitchen door, staring at the jar. Her heart pounding she took the few steps toward it and lifted the lid.

It felt as though she was stealing, and she promptly closed the lid again. Tears leaked from her eyes.

She would never see her sister or William again, and neither would Annie. She opened the lid to the cookie jar once again, and was surprised at the amount of paper money in there.

She couldn't take it. It belonged to her sister. A voice in her head told her Elizabeth was never coming back, and if she didn't take it, the money would go to strangers.

The Lord alone knew she needed that money to ensure she and Annie survived the long trip unscathed.

She reached in and pulled the bundle of notes out. She'd never seen so much money in all her life before and wondered why Elizabeth had stashed it there. Hands shaking, she replaced the lid and walked back toward her room.

She passed the master bedroom on her way. It was then she realized everything in the house needed to go. She couldn't just walk away and leave all her sister's belongings where they were.

She sat on the edge of the large bed and wept for all she had lost, and vowed this would be the last time she shed any tears. Her beautiful niece needed her, and she had to be strong.

As if on queue, Annie began to cry. Poor little mite would be wanting a bottle.

Magdalena picked the baby up, giving her an extra hug, then changed her diaper.

Their new lives would start in a little over twenty-four hours. She wondered how they would fare.

Chapter Two

"You can take all those boxes," Magdalena said sadly.

The Brotherhood for the Destitute had come to collect William and Elizabeth's clothes and shoes. Her sister had many beautiful gowns, but Magdalena knew she wouldn't be able to bring herself to wear them. She did keep Elizabeth's wedding gown though, and would be proud to wear it at her own wedding. If she ended up getting married, that was.

The furniture had come with the house, as well as all the kitchen supplies.

She'd packed up the few toys Annie had, as well as clothing that still fitted her niece. The rest had been boxed and donated as well.

When they left in the morning, the house had to be left as they'd found it – devoid of any personal items.

William's employer had visited, and pushed a small wad of notes into her hand. "Money owing for wages," he'd said, and then told her how sorry he was. The money wasn't much, but every little bit helped.

Through all this, Annie sat happily on her aunt's lap, gurgling and giggling with each new visitor. Tonight would be their last night in the home she'd enjoyed for some years, and the bed she'd come to find comfort in.

She set out warm clothes for Annie for the trip, along with a knitted cap for her little head. With a little over a month until Christmas, the weather was turning. She had no idea what it would be like on the train, but wasn't willing to take the risk.

As she climbed into bed that night, she prayed for the souls of her sister and brother-in-law. She also prayed that Mr Jacob Carruthers was an understanding man.

At precisely 10 am, Jacob put down his pencil and donned his thick woolen coat. He put his hat on his head and pulled on his gloves. "Abigail," he said as he left his office. "I am off to collect Miss Magdalena Roth from the station. I will be gone about an hour."

She nodded. He'd confided to Abigail about his change of mind, but it was far too late for regrets. He'd been brought up to understand if you made a decision, you stuck with it.

Unfortunately, this decision was life-changing. Reneging would not be a good look. But more than that, Miss Roth would be put in a precarious situation.

"A promise is a promise," he muttered under his breath as he approached the Great Falls station. It was a small station here, nowhere near as big as Dayton Falls, the next stop along. That town had been established some time before Great Falls, and had grown substantially. It was also a major station and attracted many more visitors.

Great Falls had also grown since the railway came along, and he could imagine the growth ten years down the track. It could only be good for business.

He waited impatiently on the platform for what seemed ages. Several men alighted the train, and a few couples, but no women traveling alone. She must have missed her train.

He was about to turn away and return to the bank, when a woman with a baby in a carriage stood in the middle of the platform and called his name.

"Mr Carruthers. Mr Jacob Carruthers?" she called aloud.

He gasped. This surely couldn't be Miss Roth? There was no mention of a child in her letters. He would have rejected her immediately had she mentioned it.

He pulled his coat tighter around himself and straightened his tie. "That is I," he said formally. "And you are?"

He held his breath, hoping it wasn't his intended bride.

"Miss Magdalena Roth," she answered quietly.

He stared into the carriage at the sleeping child. "You didn't mention you had a child," he said angrily.

She swallowed, and took a step back, pulling the contraption along with her. "There was an accident," she said, her voice barely audible.

"An accident?"

"I, I..." she began to explain, but he stopped her when she looked like she was about to bawl. He couldn't cope with crying women, never had been able to. That would be especially so with one he'd just met.

What on earth had he got himself into?

He would put her and the child up at the hotel for a few nights, then send them on their way. He opened his mouth to tell her as much, then thought of his sister, Jennifer. He could imagine what she would have to say.

"I'll take you to my house where we can talk privately," he said, looking about.

He wondered if Jennifer was in town today. She most likely would be, since she knew Miss Roth was arriving today and would force herself upon the unfortunate young woman.

But she knew how to handle a crisis. With five children, she had to.

"This way," he said, guiding her toward the cab he'd arrived in. He helped her up onto the cab, holding her by the waist. His anger in check now, he appreciated her curves.

He passed the baby up, then wrestled with the carriage. "Can you tie this thing down with the trunk," he asked the driver. The man did as requested.

He sat quietly next to her, studying the distraught expression on her face. He dearly wanted to ask what accident had occurred but had no intention to do so in front of the driver.

They soon arrived at his home, and went through the ritual in reverse. "This is my home," he said flippantly, helping her down with the baby in her arms.

She stared at it. "It's huge," she said quietly. "Surely you don't live here alone?"

"I most certainly do," he said sternly. *Who did she think lived with him?*

She placed the baby back in the carriage. It was then he realized he didn't know if it was a girl or boy.

He turned away. Was he even interested? He paid the driver, and pulling his keys from his pocket, unlocked the door and led them inside.

He watched as she glanced about, taking in the size of the place. To this day, he had no idea why he'd built such a mansion. He'd never intended to have children. Ever.

Between his sister and his mother, he'd given in to the pressure of building such a large house. At least it was an investment in his future should the bank ever fail.

"Sit yourself down," he said, indicating the sitting room. "I'll get your trunk. We don't want some vagabond stealing it. I'm sure you'll want to take it with you when you go."

He smiled tentatively, but Miss Roth turned deathly white at his offhand comment.

"Go?" she said softly. She spoke so quietly that she was barely audible.

He stared at her. She couldn't stay — surely she could see that? She was an unmarried woman with a child. He'd agreed to marry a spinster, he didn't agree to...this.

Besides, he had a reputation to uphold.

There was a knock at the door. "Ah, that will be my sister, Jennifer," he said, then went to answer the door. And not before time — she would know how to handle this situation.

"Thank goodness you're here," he said quietly. "We have a...problem."

Jennifer pushed her way through the door. "I'm Jennifer, Jacob's sister," she began, then stopped in her tracks when she saw the baby.

"Oh. You have a baby?" She moved closer and stared at the sleeping baby. Her face softened. "What's her name?"

Miss Roth shifted in her seat. "Annie. I tried to tell Mr Carruthers there'd been an accident, but he wouldn't let me."

His sister rounded on him. "Honestly, Jacob. What is wrong with you? Make yourself useful and put on the kettle." She turned back to Magdalena Roth. "Now my dear, tell me what happened."

Magdalena stared over the top of her cup at Jacob.

She'd poured out her heart to Jennifer, while her brother hid himself in the kitchen on the pretense of organising drinks for them all.

In the middle of all this, Annie had decided she needed a bottle and screamed at the top of her lungs. Jennifer had been an agent of calm in the midst of chaos.

"Here's what we're going to do," Jennifer announced after gulping down the last of her coffee. "Jacob, you go to the church and organise the preacher for two o'clock. I'll help Magdalena get ready for the wedding."

He stared at her. "Are you mad? I didn't sign up for a child."

"And neither did Magdalena. But here we are. Besides, when you get married, a baby usually results." She grinned at him. "This might be a little different, but it has the same result."

"I can't do this," he muttered, but turned away when Jennifer glared at him.

"I have my sister's wedding gown," Magdalena said quietly. Not that she wanted to wear it now. She wasn't sure why she salvaged it from those she gave away. It seemed a good idea at the time, but now the thought of it made her feel even more emotional.

Jennifer stood. "You go, Jacob," she said, shooing her brother out of the house. "We'll meet you at the church at two." He frowned at her but did as he was told.

"He doesn't want to marry me," Magdalena whispered. She wrapped Annie up, and tucked her into the carriage. "Do you know what time the next train leaves?" She would go to the next town up the line. She'd heard Dayton Falls was bigger than here. Perhaps she'd be more welcome there. Even if she was now unmarried spinster with a child.

"You are not leaving," Jennifer said between ground teeth. "I am quite angry with my brother right now. Always thinking only of himself." She stood and headed toward the trunk. "I assume it's in here?"

Magdalena opened the trunk, and pulled out the wedding gown, which she'd carefully laid on the top.

Jennifer looked it over and sighed. "It's beautiful," she said, her eyes sparkling. "You will look stunning in this. Jacob will change his mind when he sets eyes on you."

"As opposed to me looking like a street urchin after three days on the train?"

Jennifer grinned. "You are a bit of a mess, I must admit."

Magdalena wiped at her face, as if that would wipe all trace of soot from her.

Carrying the gown into a bedroom, she indicated the bride-to-be to follow her. Annie was sound asleep.

Jennifer laid the gown across the bed. Was this *his* room? Jacob's? It appeared to be the master bedroom, and that worried Magdalena.

"The bathroom is through here. Follow me." She took some towels out of a hall cupboard on her way through, and went into a large bathroom. It was bigger than the bedrooms back home.

Magdalena stared at the facilities in the room. "This is amazing," she said.

"I told Jacob he was going overboard when he built this place. But Father insisted he had to live up to his reputation."

"Reputation?"

Jennifer stared at her blankly. "You do know he's the banker surely?"

Magdalena shook her head. "He didn't tell me."

"Well he is. And he has standing in the community. That's why he's been behaving like an idiot."

Magdalena smiled at that. "He has been, hasn't he?"

Jennifer wholeheartedly agreed. "Right, let's get you into this nice hot bath. Take your time, and I'll look after the baby. I have five of my own, you know."

That told her a lot. She'd calmed Annie in a heartbeat, and organised her bottle without effort. "That might be you one day," she said, then grinned.

"I'm an old spinster of twenty-eight," Magdalena said. "I doubt that will happen."

"Don't sell yourself short. You're a beautiful woman. Once Jacob sees beyond his irritation, he will see that too."

Magdalena stared at the hot bath. It looked so enticing. This could be her last chance at self-indulgence before her marriage.

She had not long put on the wedding gown when she heard a gentle tap on the door.

"It's me, Jennifer."

She opened the door tentatively. "I need help with the buttons at the back, if you don't mind?"

"Oh, this is so exciting," Jennifer told her, fully animated. "I'm about to have a sister. I've gone all through life with an annoying brother, and now I have you!"

She spun Magdalena around and fastened the tiny buttons at the back of the dress. "I brought some flowers from the garden. Some for your bouquet, and some smaller ones for your hair."

Magdalena swallowed back a sob. It was the sort of thing her sister would have done for her. "Thank you," she said, emotion evident in her voice.

"Don't you dare cry!" Jennifer hugged her tight. "You can't get married with puffy red eyes." She pushed her new sister away. "It's almost time to leave. Hopefully my dear brother has organized a cab for us."

They walked slowly toward the sitting room. She could see Annie was still sound asleep.

"I'll carry her. That way we can leave the baby carriage here. Oh, you're going to need a crib."

Jennifer waved her hands in the air. "That's the least of your problems right now."

The driver helped her up into the cab when it arrived, then Jennifer passed Annie up, then climbed up herself. She reminded Magdalena of her own sister a lot, but was much more assertive. Bossy even. The thought made her smile.

They soon arrived at the church. It wasn't as big as the one back home, but Great Falls was no where as big as her home town.

The cab driver helped the women down, and was soon on his way. Magdalena moved tentatively toward the church doors. If the situations were reversed, would she agree to the marriage?

She wasn't sure.

She worried her bottom lip. Would she even find Mr Jacob Carruthers, Banker, Pillar of Society, waiting inside? Her heart skipped a beat. If he wasn't there, she would go back to his house and collect her belongings, then catch the next train out of town.

As Jennifer opened the big ornate doors for her, she swallowed. "I feel ill," she whispered. "And a little light-headed."

"Everything will be alright," Jennifer whispered back, reaching out to support her.

Magdalena nodded, but she wasn't convinced. "I'm scared he might not be here," she said softly.

Jennifer craned her neck and stared toward the front of the church. "Oh he's here alright. He wouldn't dare not to be."

Magdalena froze, then took her first steps toward being a married woman.

Chapter Three

Jacob's heart beat rapidly. Was he really doing this? Would he really marry a woman with a child he was unaware of?

Evidently, yes.

He looked to the preacher for support. He'd attended this church for his entire life, and Preacher Jones knew him well.

They talked quietly as they waited for the two women to arrive. Jacob checked his pocketwatch. One fifty-five. They should be here any moment. He hoped Magdalena was punctual. He insisted on punctuality.

"Your parents would be so proud," the preacher said. "They are here in spirit, if not in body," he added.

"Thank you, Preacher," Jacob said softly. He wished they were here. His father especially had helped him get to where he was today. "I miss them dearly."

Preacher Jones reached out and held his hand, then patted it. "Unfortunately, accidents happen," he said, then his head shot up. "Ah, here is your lovely bride now."

Jacob turned to see his bride walking down the aisle. Was this really the same woman? She looked beautiful. At least she'd cleaned up. She was the epitome of a grubby gypsy earlier.

He slapped himself mentally. That wasn't really fair. She'd literally just stepped off the train, and was splattered in soot. The damned stuff was on her clothes, and smudged across her face.

But now?

He stared. He couldn't help himself. This was the face of an angel. A beautiful angel.

He knew he shouldn't have such thoughts in church, and dragged his eyes away from her. His sister came behind her carrying the child.

He hadn't told the preacher about her, and wondered what he would say.

"Is the child yours, Jacob?" he asked, a frown on his face.

"What? No," he said, shocked. "It's her niece. The parents were killed in a tragic accident earlier this week."

The preacher looked at him thoughtfully. "That is so kind of you to take on someone else's child."

He stared at the preacher. He had no intention of telling him it was under duress from his constantly annoying sister.

Was he kind? He wasn't sure. The way he'd behaved when he first saw her certainly didn't prove kindness. More aggravation than anything.

Magdalena came to stand by his side. She looked even more beautiful up close. She had flowers in her hair, no doubt his sister's idea.

He leaned in and whispered. "You look beautiful," then wondered why he'd done so.

She stared into his eyes. Hers were the deepest brown he'd ever seen. They were the color of rich chocolate, and he could easily get lost in them.

"Ahem." Preacher Jones cleared his throat. "Are we ready to begin?"

Magdalena nodded.

"I think we are, Preacher Jones." Jacob automatically reached out and held her hand. He hadn't intended to do it, but he felt compelled to do so.

He felt the heat of his sister's eyes on his back. It was all he could do to not turn around and glare at her.

The vibration of his bride's shaking hand as he held it gutted him. He squeezed her hand, trying to reassure her.

What was wrong with him? Nothing was going to plan. He was meant to be back at work two hours ago, not standing here in the damned church preparing to marry.

When he realized he'd cussed in church, even if it was in his mind, he closed his eyes and prayed for forgiveness.

"Do you Jacob Carruthers, take this woman, Magdalena Roth for your wife?"

His eyes flashed open, and he turned to look at her. Her eyes pleaded with him and he knew it was too late to back out. "I do."

"And do you Magdalena Roth take this man, Jacob Carruthers for your husband?"

"I do."

When the preacher said the part about kissing his bride, his heart skipped. She was so beautiful, this wife of his, and he was sure she'd be very kissable too.

He cupped his hands on either side of her face, and leaned in to kiss her. Their lips met, oh so gently, and she pulled back slightly as though she hadn't expected it.

He leaned in again, and kissed her more fully this time. When he eventually pulled back his lips were tingling.

He stared down at her. At this petite woman who stood next to him, who was now his legally wedded wife.

She put her fingers to her lips.

Jennifer moved forward with the baby. "Congratulations!" she said, kissing and hugging them both. "Let's go back to your place, Jacob, then we can organize a celebration dinner."

He inwardly groaned. *Would this never end?*

Jacob helped the women down from the cab.

As he held his bride around the waist, their eyes met. There was something about her eyes — they got to him each and every time.

He quickly pulled his gaze away and placed her gently on the ground. He turned to the cab driver and shoved some notes into his hand. The convenience of having the man hang around for the duration was worth the extra money.

He unlocked the door, and Jennifer rushed in ahead of them, holding tight to little Annie, hugging her lovingly. "My new little niece," he heard her whisper not so quietly in the child's ear.

He waited for Magdalena to step inside when he noticed his sister glaring at him. It took him a moment, but he finally realized what she was trying to tell him.

He swooped his bride up and carried her across the threshold.

She let out a yelp of surprise, but wrapped her arms around his neck. It felt nice. Their faces were so close he could feel her warm breath on his cheek, then she rested her head against his shoulder – as though she needed someone to support her. And he supposed she did – she'd been through so much lately.

It evoked a reaction he couldn't decipher. He'd never felt like this before with a woman. He'd taken women out on dates, but they were mostly vipers looking for an easy life. Most especially, they were after his money.

He shuddered at the thought.

Miss Magdalena Roth, correction, Mrs Jacob Carruthers, had no knowledge of his wealth until today. Which made it even better.

All he had to do now was ensure she didn't get her hands on it.

He strolled into the sitting room and gently put her on her feet. "You took me by surprise," she said softly.

As he settled her on the carpeted floor, her perfume drifted into his nostrils. He breathed it in, then checked himself. He needed to keep his distance.

He didn't want this marriage, and he wasn't going to let some wisp of a woman change his mind. He straightened up, then pulled his jacket back into position.

"You need a crib for the baby." Jennifer was renowned for saying things out of the blue.

"A crib? Where on earth am I to get a crib at this short notice?" Honestly, did she think he was a miracle worker?

"There's one sitting unused at my place. You can pick it up later."

Did she really expect him to go out there today? He'd already lost almost a full day's work. "Can't Charles..."

"No. He's busy, and can't afford to take the time off. We're not loaded like you." She winked across to Magdalena who stood there taking in the whole crazy conversation.

"We still have to organize the wedding dinner," Jennifer said. "And you're not going to be stingy about it. This is the only wedding Maggie will get. She deserves to be treated special."

"Maggie? Do you mean Magdalena?" His sister was incredibly irritating at times. He looked toward his new wife, but she was grinning at the goings on. How terribly frustrating.

Jennifer laughed so hard she snorted.

"It isn't funny," he said, totally offended.

She handed off the baby to Magdalena. "Right. I'm off to organize the dinner. Jacob, you help Maggie unpack and hang her clothes."

Without giving him a chance to response, she left them alone. "But..." Too late, she was gone.

He glanced across at his new wife. "Do what you need to do with the child, then we'll get you sorted."

He stormed into the kitchen and stoked the stove. No doubt Jennifer would want a coffee when she returned. Whenever that might be.

He filled the kettle and set out the mugs, then pottered around doing basically nothing. Anything to fill the void while his wife sorted the child.

His wife. Would he ever get used to that? He didn't think so.

He returned to the sitting room to find the child on the floor, a banana in her hand, his Magdalena sitting nearby on the sofa. "She's hungry," he was told. Didn't babies only have milk? He thought back to his nieces and nephews, and realized at this age they were eating some foods.

He made a mental note to get a high chair. He couldn't allow the child to sit on the floor to eat – it wasn't hygienic. Jacob wasn't sure what else they'd need, but he'd ask his sister. If she was living under his roof, he would attend to her needs.

"I'm afraid I'll have to do some washing," Magdalena told him. "I'm running short of diapers."

"Did you not bring enough?" Now he was getting annoyed.

Her chin went up. "I brought all my sister had available." She stood abruptly. "Everything happened a little over twenty-four hours before I was due to leave to come here. It was not planned. I was not supposed to bring my niece – it was to be only me." Her face was getting redder, the more she spoke. "I had two choices – bring her with me, or leave her in an orphanage. That wasn't about to happen." She turned away from him. "I'm very sorry. We'll leave if you would prefer."

Her shoulders were shaking as she stood with her back to him.

Hell, now he'd made her cry. That didn't sit well with him, not to mention what his sister would say when she got back.

He stepped tentatively toward her, then put his arm up around her shoulders. She swung into him and cried into his chest. He didn't know what to do except put his arms around her and give comfort.

What would he have done in her situation? No doubt he would make the same choice – he wouldn't leave his nieces or nephews behind, given the same circumstances.

Without permission, his arms suddenly had a life of their own, and he began rubbing her back.

What was wrong with him?

"I, I'm sorry," she said between sobs. "It's just…"

He looked down into her red blotchy face. "You've been through a lot," he said quietly.

He continued to comfort her. He couldn't begin to imagine what she'd been through the past few days. She'd not only lost her sister and brother-in-law, she'd inherited a child that was not her own.

Yes, the child was her niece, but you don't expect to have to take on that level of responsibility. Especially without warning.

She stopped shaking. Did that mean she'd stopped crying?

She looked up at him, her pretty face marred by red eyes. "I'm really sorry," she said softly. "I, I think it just all got too much."

He left his arms where they were. It felt good to him, and he thought it would help to comfort her a little longer.

His fingers played against her soft cheek. "I won't send you away," he said gently. "You're my wife. We'll work it out."

She hiccupped then rested her head against his chest again. "Thank you." His arms tightened around her.

His interfering sister chose that very moment to walk through the door. "Everything is organized," she began, then grinned.

He waved his hand across in front of himself in an effort to stop her in her tracks. Magdalena pulled away then ran up the stairs.

Her grin changed to a grimace. "What did you do?" She was beyond irritated and blamed him for the upset.

"Keep your voice down," he said between gritted teeth. "I think it's all become too much. The shock of losing her family seems to have finally hit her."

"Perhaps I'll make sure she's alright?" Jennifer seemed uncertain how to handle this situation. It was new to both of them.

"I'm sure that's a brilliant idea. But what about the child?" They both looked to the floor. She was making a huge mess with the banana – squeezing it between her fingers. More was going on her clothes than in her mouth.

He grimaced at the mess.

"Get used to it Jacob. This is life as a parent."

He glared at her. "A parent? I'm not her parent. I'm nothing to this child."

Jennifer glared back. "She has a name. Annie. And whether or not you want to believe it, you are now effectively her father."

She leaned down and cleaned the child up the best she could, then stormed off to check on Magdalena. "Keep an eye on her," she said, as she disappeared into the hall.

He found a toy in the carriage, and handed it to the child. Er, Annie. She reached for it, then played happily with it.

If only it would always be that easy.

Chapter Four

She stared at herself in the mirror.

Her face was red and blotchy. Magdalena couldn't remember the last time she'd cried like this. To do it in front of a total stranger was abhorrent – even if that stranger was now her husband.

She heard a soft tap on the bathroom door. "Can I come in?" Jennifer's voice came clearly through the door.

She gazed at herself in the mirror again. "I guess so." She was a total mess and wanted to crawl into a hole.

Tears welled in her eyes again. She was certain she was all cried out, but then the vision of her sister drowning crossed her mind. A sob forced its way out, and she had no way of stopping it.

"You poor thing," Jennifer said gently. "Here's a facecloth. Put some cold water on it, and put it to your face."

Magdalena stared at her. "It will help alleviate the redness."

She did as she was told. It did help, but more than anything, it made her feel a little better. "Is Annie alright?" She hoped so.

"I told Jacob to look after her."

Magdalena gasped. "I'd better go." She was about to leave when Jennifer stopped her.

"It will do him good. Let him get used to her."

She sank down into the padded chair near the ornate mirror. "I shouldn't have come here. I've put you all in a bad position."

Jennifer moved closer, then put her arm around her new sister-in-law. "What would you have done? Where would you have lived? You can't work with a baby, so how would you have supported the two of you?"

She was right. About everything. Apart from anything else, she would have been kicked out of the house. With William dead, the house would be passed on to his replacement.

She swallowed back a sob, and at the floor. "I don't know," she said slightly above a whisper.

Jennifer wet the cloth again and handed it to her. "Wash your face again, then have a lay down. You must be exhausted."

Magdalena nodded. "I am tired after that long trip. But Annie…"

"I'll look after Annie. You need to rest." She was led into the bedroom where she'd changed earlier. "Lay down, and I'll come back later."

She was certain she wouldn't sleep, but pulled off her boots and did as she was told. Once she closed her eyes, she was soon fast asleep.

When her eyes finally flickered open, she was confused. She had no idea where she was. Looking around, the room was unfamiliar, and she gasped in fright.

She quickly sat up, and balanced on the edge of the bed. It was then she looked down and saw the wedding gown. Everything came rushing back.

That was not necessarily a good thing.

She went to the window and looked out. The sky was darkening. How long had she been asleep?

Rushing to the door, she pulled it open only to find Jacob standing there, about to knock. "Ah, you're awake."

She wanted to crawl into a hole. Her embarrassment was overwhelming. "I'm sorry about earlier," she said quietly, avoiding looking into his face.

He reached out and gently grasped her chin, forcing her to look at him. "Don't apologize. You've endured so much lately."

For someone who didn't want her there, his forgiveness was complexing.

"It's almost time for us to leave for this wretched wedding dinner," he said, his annoyance evident.

She frowned.

"It's not that I don't want to celebrate. Not really. It's just that I have no idea who my sister has dragged along to this wretched affair." He grinned. "She can be a nuisance at times, that sister of mine."

She looked down at her crumpled gown. "I'll have to change," she said quietly. "Hopefully my other gowns are not in the same state."

"Before you do that, come with me, there's something I want to show you."

He led her down the hall and into another bedroom. Jacob put his fingers to his lips. "She's been asleep for sometime. Jennifer put her down."

Annie lay asleep in a beautifully made crib. She was wrapped in pretty blankets that Magdalena had never seen before. "How?"

"Jennifer and I slipped out and collected the crib while you slept. Annie came with us. She was a hit with my nieces and nephews." He smiled for probably the first time today. "They love their new cousin."

Did that mean everything would be alright? She didn't dare hope for a good outcome at this point.

He reached for her chin again. "Magdalena," he said softly, forcing her to look at him. "We'll work it out, I'm certain of it."

She nodded, but wasn't so sure.

"We got off to a bad start. I'm sorry – it was such a shock to see you with a baby."

She could totally understand that. The past days had been a shock to her. If true be told, she was still in shock over the loss of Elizabeth and William. Not to mention finding herself an instant mother to her niece.

"You didn't sign up for any of this," she said quietly. So softly her voice was barely audible.

"No, but we're married now. You're my wife, and I'll take care of you both."

"Thank you," she said, then moved close to him and put her arms around him. He hesitated at first, but then she felt his arms slip around her back.

She could stand there like that forever. She felt so comfortable and so safe with him. These last days she'd felt very unsafe. Especially on the train with strangers all around her.

Annie suddenly began to cry. Jacob's arms slid from around her, and she felt suddenly bereft. Which was ridiculous. They'd known each other less than twenty-four hours and she already felt a connection to him, albeit very small. Did he feel the same?

She lifted the baby out of her crib, and was immediately reward with a hug. Poor Annie, she must be confused about where her parents were, and where she was. It had been hard enough for her, and she understood what was going on. A baby of this age couldn't possibly understand.

"Let's get you changed and fed." She glanced around the room. "Where did all those diapers come from?" She was confused. She only had a handful of clean diapers left.

"I bought them. Jennifer was a big help – she knew exactly what you would need. There are a few other items in the cupboard."

Magdalena put Annie back in the crib while she checked it out. "Thank you," she said quietly. "I don't know what to say."

"You just said it. We'll get more when you know what is required."

She took Annie from the crib again and began to change her. Her life had taken a totally different turn. She was yet to find out if that was good or bad.

Jacob sat back and studied the room.

There weren't as many people at the wedding reception as he'd envisaged. Just a handful of close friends and family. And of course his secretary Abigail.

Magdalena sat beside him looking petrified. And why shouldn't she? She didn't know these people. She knew Jennifer of course, but both his sister and himself were almost complete strangers to her.

It was less than twelve hours since they'd met. He gazed at her thoughtfully. The baby carriage sat next to her — she'd made it abundantly clear she wouldn't let the child out of her sight.

And who could blame her? Surrounded by strangers, and in an unknown environment. He would be the same if it was his child.

That made him pause.

In effect it was his child. Perhaps not by blood, but certainly by marriage.

His head shot up when a chair scraped across the floor. "Thank you all for coming tonight." His brother-in-law Charles stood with a glass of champagne in his hand. "I'd like to invite you all to join me in a toast."

He lifted the glass to the guests. "To Jacob and Magdalena. May your marriage be long and fruitful."

He turned to Jacob and winked. His wife blushed and slid down in her seat. He glared at Charles who's only response was to grin. The man could be so unrefined at times.

Reaching across, he snatched up Magdalena's hand and squeezed it. "Take no notice," he whispered. "He thinks he's funny, but he's not."

She nodded, but still looked embarrassed.

As their guests toasted them, Jacob stood. "I'd like to make a toast too," he said, still holding his wife's hand. "To my beautiful wife. It may not have been the start we'd expected, but things can only get better."

"To Magdalena."

"We are also welcoming her niece into our family. Due to tragic circumstances, Annie will be living with us."

He heard the gasps from their guests. It was better it was out in the open than to have unfounded rumors abound.

Before anyone could say or do anything, the meals were served. Jacob was certain this was the easy part. Making this marriage work would be the most difficult thing by far.

She hadn't expected Jacob to announce Annie as part of their new family. He seemed to have an issue with her, but perhaps it was a case of her being unexpected.

She was still walking around stunned with the events of the past days. It was less than a week since the tragic accident, since she'd had to assume the position of mother to her niece.

It was definitely a struggle, and she prayed it would get easier. More than anything, she prayed that Jacob would assume the role of father.

The way things stood right now, that didn't seem possible. He rarely called her Annie, instead, preferring to call her *the child*.

Jennifer warned her it might take time. Her brother was thirty-four years old, and had been a confirmed bachelor since his teenage years.

He'd always vowed never to marry, and never have children. He only tolerated her children because they were family. She was almost positive of it.

She didn't say this to put him in a bad light, Jennifer explained. Only to clarify his strange behavior when it came to Annie.

Magdalena didn't know what to make of it.

After having a bottle, Annie had slept through most of the dinner. The train trip had no doubt exhausted her.

Jacob had arranged for a cab to take them home. She wondered what would happen after that. She hoped he would give her some time to get used to being his wife. As a spinster, she'd had no experience whatsoever with men – that wasn't necessarily a good thing.

When they arrived back to Jacob's house, he quickly jumped down and pulled the baby carriage off the back of the cab. She passed Annie down, and he put her in the contraption.

Then he lifted his wife down.

She shivered as he held her by the waist and looked up into her eyes. Their faces were very close, and she thought he might kiss her. Until the driver cleared his throat. Then the moment was lost.

He frowned, then carefully placed her on the ground.

He shoved some notes into the cab driver's hand, then moved toward the door, unlocking it.

"Would you like some coffee," she asked when they were safely inside.

"I can do that," he said. "You sort out the child."

The child. The child! Would he ever use her actual name? "Her name is Annie," she ground out, and he glared at her.

"I know that," he said, as if there was not an issue. "Get her settled, and I'll make the coffee."

She left quickly, not wanting to wake Annie. If she was left undisturbed, she should sleep through to the morning.

She lifted her carefully out of the carriage and into the crib, covering her with the pretty blankets Jennifer had kindly left.

She quietly left the room, and returned to the kitchen. He handed her a coffee.

"Tell me a little about yourself," he said, looking over the top of his coffee mug. "Something you didn't mention in your letter."

She nodded. "I'm a teacher. I think I told you that?" She had, he told her. "I lost my job recently," she said. "They decided to put a man in my position, simply because he was a man."

"That doesn't seem fair."

She agreed. "No it's not. As a single woman, I had to support myself, just as a man would have to."

They chatted a little about his job and his standing in the community. "As my wife, I expect you to attend certain events in town. The child complicates things."

"Annie is not a complication," she said adamantly. "She is my niece. An innocent child. None of this is of her doing." She slammed down her mug harder on the table than she meant to, and stood abruptly.

Would he ever accept Annie was part of her? Annie was important to her, and she would ensure she was safe and happy at all cost.

He stood with her. "I didn't mean it like that."

"Yes you did," she accused him, certain she was correct. "I'm not sure what I'm meant to do. I've explained the situation in great detail. I don't want to have to explain it all again." She was so angry, she was shaking. What did she have to do to get through to him?

He took two strides toward her and held her tight. "I just meant we would have to find a sitter. Some of these events don't allow children."

It felt nice to be held, and soon she'd stopped shaking. But she still wasn't sure he wanted them both. Things would have to change or this marriage was not going to work for either of them.

What she would do then, she didn't know.

She was convinced he wasn't interested in her at all, perhaps didn't even like her, but rested her head against his chest. She was so tired, and so much in need of comfort right now.

His heart was beating rapidly almost in time with her own.

She took a deep breath, and looked up into his face. His eyes were the blue of the sky on a sunny day, and they drew her in. He stared into her eyes, and she was mesmerized by him. She couldn't pull her gaze away.

His hand came up and gently cupped her chin, then his face came slowly toward hers, his eyes staring at her mouth.

She licked her lips.

At first his kiss was like the touch of a butterfly's wings. It was soft and gentle, and was gone almost before she knew it was there.

She stood on her toes in an effort to get closer to him, and his head came down again. This time he pushed her dress aside at the shoulder and kissed her bare skin, then gently kissed her neck.

His breathing got quicker, and he suddenly moved from her neck to her lips. It was a tender kiss, but not as tender as the earlier kiss. This one was more urgent, and she was surprised at her need to kiss him too.

She had no idea she could feel this way, especially for someone she'd only just met. She wondered if he felt the same, or whether it was simply a case of manly urges.

Without warning, he swept her off her feet and carried her to the marriage bed.

Chapter Five

Jacob awoke as the sun rose. That was nothing new for him. But today was different.

Today was the first day of his marriage.

He looked down into the face of the angel who slept soundly in his bed. He enjoyed waking up to her pretty face this morning, and knew he could easily get used to it.

She was hesitant last night – they both were – but now that first night was over, things could only improve.

He was trying to decide whether or not to wake her when the child began to wail. He glanced down into Magdalena's face – she didn't so much as stir. She'd been through so much lately, and was surely exhausted.

Without hesitation, he pulled on a robe and went to the nursery as he'd now deemed it.

His heart did a little flip-flop when he noticed she was trying to pull herself up out of the crib. He let out the breath he didn't know he was holding when she couldn't manage it.

Standing next to the crib, the smell was almost overwhelming. Hesitating, he reached into the cupboard and pulled out a diaper. He lifted the child out of the crib and lay her on the floor.

He stared into the angelic face. She stared up at him. Her brown eyes matched those of her aunt. Her little hands reached out to touch him, and she looped her tiny fingers around one of his.

His heart melted.

For about twenty seconds, then he shook himself. He had no right to get attached to this child. He didn't know her, he didn't know her mother.

He just needed to get on with the job. It was then he realized he had no idea how to fold a diaper.

Jacob groaned. He'd seen his sister do this a thousand times – surely a mere diaper was not going to get the better of him?

He opened the wet diaper, then cringed. Not only was it wet, there was a nasty package inside as well.

He held his nose, then realized he couldn't change the diaper while holding his nose. He needed to get this over with as quickly as he could, and folded it as best he could.

That had to be the most disgusting thing he'd ever had to do.

He picked her up when she was finally changed, and the baby leaned into him and wrapped her little arms around his neck.

He was about to pull her back, when she dropped a sloppy kiss on his unshaven face. His heart kicked up a notch.

She leaned back and stared into his eyes, and her little hands rubbed his other cheek. Then she hugged him again.

He hadn't signed up for this. What was he to do?

Left with no other choice, he wrapped his arms around the child. She snuggled back into his neck.

"Good morning."

Magdalena stood in the doorway watching their every move, her hair ruffled and her cheeks pink. The child's arms reached for her. "Mag, Mag," she said in her baby talk.

He handed her over.

The diaper slipped off in the process. Magdalena laughed. "Thank you for trying, but it doesn't seem to have worked very well."

She lay the child on the floor and reworked the diaper. "Where are the safety pins?"

"What? Oh." He reached for them from the top of the cupboard. "Sorry, I didn't want her to get hold of them, then forgot about them."

She laughed. "No wonder the diaper fell off."

He felt deflated. He managed a bank and all it entailed on a daily basis – how could he mess up such a simple task as changing a diaper?

"Don't worry about it. You'll get used to it."

Would he? The likelihood of that happening was pretty slim.

"What time do you start work," she asked in her half-asleep voice.

"What? Oh, I told Abigail I'd only be in for a few hours later today. I thought we could spend a bit of time getting to know each other better."

She smiled. "That would be nice. Thank you," she said quietly. "Perhaps you could show me around town?"

The child began to wail again.

"She's hungry. I'll organise her bottle." She reached across and handed the baby to him. "I won't be long."

What did she expect him to do with the child? Entertain her? If she did, he had no idea how to achieve that.

"Wait," he called after her, but she was gone. Instead he carried the baby into the kitchen where he found Magdalena. "What am I supposed to do with her?"

Magdalena turned, and he caught sight of her pink lips. He wanted more of her, and stepped closer, the baby still in his arms.

"Put her on the floor in the sitting room. She'll be fine there."

He hesitated, not sure it was the best place for her.

"We'll have to child-proof everything," she called from the kitchen.

Child-proof? He liked his house just as it was. What other sacrifices did she expect him to make?

He stormed into the kitchen, ready to have it out with his wife, when he heard paper ripping.

Jacob went running back to investigate. He froze. His financial periodicals that had taken months to arrive were in shreds.

She'd pulled herself up onto the low table where he'd left them. Twenty-four hours ago he had no inkling such a risk existed.

He stood over the baby and scolded her, taking the torn pages from her. She began to wail. Loudly.

Magdalena came running in. "What happened?" she asked urgently.

"This is what happened," he answered angrily, holding up the shredded pages.

She took the damaged periodicals from him. "It's just paper. Oh look, she's standing. She's never done that before."

He was angry, and she was delighted. Jacob sat on the edge of the sofa. What sort of predicament had he gotten himself into?

All he'd wanted was a bride, not a family. He put his head in his hands - his head was pounding.

He suddenly stood. "Coffee," he said abruptly. "I need coffee. I can't cope with all of this."

She stared at him, perplexed. Did she not understand the dilemma he was in? That *she'd* put him in?

"What exactly is your problem," she asked, hands on her hips.

She looked kind of cute, standing there, defying him. But now was not the time for such thoughts. "If you really want to know, it's you – and the child. I, I didn't expect all this."

She glared at him. "Don't worry," she said, tears welling in her eyes. "We'll be gone by the end of the day."

She reached down and lifted the child. "Come on, Annie. We know when we're not wanted."

"But..." She was gone before he had a chance to explain.

He felt like a heel. It wasn't that he didn't want them there, not really. At least that's what he told himself.

What he needed was time to get used to this change of situation.

Magdalena seemed like a nice person. The child seemed well behaved – most of the time. The more he thought about it, the more he realized the damaged magazines were his fault, and even inconsequential in the scheme of things.

Jennifer had warned him yesterday, but he hadn't listened. She'd said it would take time; he'd brushed her words aside.

He stormed into the kitchen and stoked the fire, then filled the kettle. A mug of coffee would definitely calm his nerves and hopefully send his headache scurrying.

Setting out the mugs, he tried to remember how Magdalena took her coffee. Was it black or white? With or without sugar?

He closed his eyes and tried to remember.

Damn it, he couldn't think. He was so upset with what had occurred this morning, and he didn't know how to move beyond it.

The kettle boiled and he went to the bedroom to check on the pair. He'd expected them back by now. Magdalena lay on the bed with her back to him, with the child by her side.

"What are we going to do, Annie," he heard her ask quietly. "We have to leave."

He heard her sniffle. He'd upset her dreadfully, and felt like a rat. "Don't leave," he said softly. "I don't want you to go."

68

She turned to face him, tears still in her eyes. "Is that true, or are you just saying that?"

His heart ached. He'd never intended to upset anyone, especially not his new wife.

He came to sit on the side of the bed next to her. "I'm sorry," he said. "This is such a different situation for me."

She nodded, but didn't say a word.

"I expected a bride, not a family."

She glared at him.

"Damn it," he said under his breath. He was not explaining himself well. "I didn't mean it the way it came out," he said, feeling more than a little ashamed of himself.

He pulled her up into his arms. "I truly am sorry," he said again, not sure if he was trying to convince himself or Magdalena. "Can we start over?"

She looked up at him, concern in her eyes. "I, I guess," she said, quite obviously not convinced.

"The kettle has boiled. I went to make coffee, but I don't know how you have it," he said, totally changing the subject.

She stared at him. Had he done the wrong thing bringing up coffee? Being married was far different to what he'd expected.

"White with two sugars," she said softly. Her hand went to his cheek, and it felt good.

He leaned in and lightly kissed her lips, then she rested her head against his chest. The last twenty-four hours had turned his life upside down.

He wondered what would happen in the next twenty-four.

Magdalena pushed the carriage across the boardwalk, Jacob walking next to her. Annie was no longer content laying down in her carriage, and persisted in sitting up, taking in her new environment.

Jacob glanced down at Annie and frowned. Was he unhappy? She wasn't certain.

Magdalena stole her attention from Jacob, and glanced around at the array of businesses available in this little township – barber, butcher, dressmaker, boot store, and many more. Not to mention the heart of every town, the Mercantile.

Jacob led her toward the store. "We need to stock up on supplies," he said, as he held the door open for her.

"Morning, Cecil," Jacob said as a man around thirty approached them. "This is my wife,

Magdalena. Anything she wants, put on my account."

The man smiled. "Certainly, Jacob." He turned to Magdalena. "Pleased to meet you Mrs Carruthers."

She smiled at him. He seemed pleasant enough, and was well-dressed in his black suit with a collared shirt and tie, a crisp white apron over the top of it all. She glanced toward the floor – shiny black boots.

Her father always said you could tell the caliber of a man by the way he dressed.

She turned to her husband – his attire was almost identical. That elicited a grin from her. Her father would have approved.

"What can I do for you today, Jacob?"

"We need more diapers, as well as clothes for the child."

Magdalena frowned. "More diapers? I can wash clothes you know," she whispered.

"Follow me." Cecil led them to a corner of the store. "Here are the baby clothes. There's not a huge choice, but I can order in whatever you need."

"What about a stroller? Do you carry those?" Jacob's words surprised her, and she glanced up at him.

"We can make do with the carriage," she protested.

"We will not *make do*," he said. "Annie will have a new stroller, she deserves the best."

Annie? He used her name – was this some sort of break-through? She dare not hope.

"Make sure it's top quality. We'll also take four baby bottles and nipples." He looked to his wife. "Do we need formula too?" She nodded. "Order in two cans of baby formula for now."

He put his arm around Magdalena who was feeling very uncertain about all the money he was spending. "What shall we have for supper tonight?"

At least that was an area where she felt comfortable. "I could make a hearty vegetable soup?"

He grinned. "That sounds excellent. Get whatever you need. I'm sure the pantry will be empty."

She frowned. "You don't know?"

Jacob shrugged. "I had a lady coming in to clean and cook, but she married recently and stopped coming."

She would make an extra effort with his supper tonight. He'd probably lived on beans and bacon for ages. She reached for flour, sugar, butter, milk, an array of vegetables, as well as a variety of staples. He added the items to a box he'd procured from the Mercantile owner.

"I think we're done?" he queried Magdalena.

"Yes, I think so. I guess I can always come back if I need to."

Annie became restless as they headed toward the counter, and Magdalena picked her up. Without warning, Jacob stopped when he spotted something, but she wasn't sure what it was.

Until he held it out in front of himself. "What do you think? Do you like it?" he asked Annie, dangling a small doll in front of her. She reached out and grinned at him. He handed her the toy.

"You're going to spoil her," Magdalena said, secretly happy that he seemed to finally be warming to the baby.

He dropped the box on the counter, then reached out for the baby. "Any chance of having it all delivered, Cecil?"

It was a bit much to carry back to the house, Magdalena conceded. "I'll need some of these early enough to prepare supper," she said. "Soup takes quite a while to cook."

Once she'd put aside her immediate ingredients, the rest were earmarked for delivery.

Jacob put Annie back in the carriage, then took the small box of groceries she required.

Standing outside the door he pointed to a building across the road. "There's the bank," he said proudly.

"It looks nice." She wasn't sure what else to say. A bank was nothing fancy, after all.

"We'll cross over and you can see the other businesses," he told her. "We'll call at the bakery and get some bread for luncheon."

When they got to the edge of the boardwalk, Jacob reached down with his free hand and lifted the end of the carriage. Magdalena followed suit.

The dirt road was littered with ruts and it would have been a bumpy ride for little Annie. She was grateful for his foresight.

As they reached the other side, he gently placed the carriage down on the boardwalk. As they went to move off Magdalena shivered.

Her actions didn't go unnoticed. "Cold?" he asked, frowning. She nodded. "It's coming on for Christmas. The cold weather is setting in. It won't be long it will be snowing."

Her eyes opened wide. "Snowing? Really?" She grinned, she couldn't help herself. "I've never seen snow before."

"You're in for a treat, then." She wasn't sure, but felt he was being sarcastic.

She rubbed her hands together. They suddenly felt chilled. "Really?"

"No, not really. It's dreadful stuff. Cold, wet, and slippery. It's the bane of my existence at times. Some days I can't even get out of the house because of the horrid mess."

"Oh."

He suddenly stopped. "Here we are at the bakery."

They went inside and he introduced her to the owner, then bought their supplies.

Annie began to wail. "She's probably wet and hungry. And tired," Magdalena said. Jacob picked up the doll that was laying in the carriage, and handed it back to Annie.

"Here," he said. "Amuse yourself with this for a few minutes. We'll be home soon."

She snatched it out of his hands and cuddled it tightly. He grinned. "She seems to like the doll," he said.

"She does." Her little eyes began to flutter closed, and she lay back and promptly fell asleep.

Jacob glanced at her. "That was sudden."

"It's been a big day. In fact, it's been a big week – for both of us. That train trip took a lot out of me too."

He put his free arm around her and pulled her close. It felt nice, but was it all for show? People shuffled about the town, going about their business, and Jacob would want them all to know he cared about his new wife.

They reached the end of the boardwalk, and he let go to grab hold of the carriage again. He lifted it carefully down, and they continued their walk back to his house.

"Did you enjoy our trip to town?" he asked quietly, in an effort not to wake the baby.

She nodded.

"You can go there any time you want," he said. "You don't have to ask permission."

She just might take him up on that. It was a pleasant stroll to the shops, especially on a nice day. Even better with her husband tagging along with them.

He carried the supplies into the kitchen while Magdalena sorted Annie. She managed to change the baby's diaper without her waking, then carefully placed her in the crib.

She was looking forward to sitting down with a nice mug of coffee and a few minutes to herself. She'd just sat down at the table, when the wailing began. She put her hands to her face. "I don't think I can do this," she said to her husband sitting beside her.

"We'll work it out," he said, snatching up the bottle she'd already prepared. "You drink your coffee. I'll sort out the child."

He'd reverted back to calling Annie *the child* again. Would things ever improve, or would they be moving on after all?

Chapter Six

Jacob left for work soon after luncheon. They had jam sandwiches, since there was nothing else to put in them. Neither of them had thought of that when they were at the Mercantile.

Magdalena walked to the front door with him, Annie in her arms. He leaned in and kissed her on the cheek, then Annie reached out her little arms to him.

He held her and pulled her close, and two little arms snaked around his neck. Magdalena watched with disappointment as he grimaced at the action.

Annie leaned back and stared into his face. "I have to go, little one," he said, still avoiding using her name.

She looked as though she might cry, but waved instead. He grinned as he handed her back.

"I'll probably be late. I have a lot to catch up on," he said, as he prepared to leave the house.

Magdalena wrinkled her nose. "It doesn't matter, I guess. It's only soup."

He leaned in and kissed her again, only this time lightly on the lips, as though this was the most natural thing for him to do.

After he left, she carried Annie inside. "I have to prepare the soup," she told Annie sternly. "You need to behave yourself."

She rummaged through the cupboards and found a large pot to make the soup in. Investigating further she found a chopping board and a number of smaller pots in another cupboard.

She placed the chopping board on the counter top then pulled the vegetables out of the box and began to peel and chop them. When they were finally ready, she threw them into the pot, adding water, then put them on the stove.

Annie had amused herself with the doll all this time, but now was getting restless. It was distracting Magdalena from what she was doing.

Then she remembered the lids to the pots, and gave them to Annie – it didn't take long before she realized smashing them together made a wonderful noise.

A wonderfully loud noise.

It kept her happy – for now at least.

While the soup bubbled away on the stove, Magdalena inspected the pantry – there was little of any merit there. What she did find either looked or smelled terrible, or was full of weevils. It all ended up in the rubbish.

A total clean-out was what that pantry needed, and that's exactly what it got. She swept and dusted, then washed down all the shelves using soap and water before filling the clean shelves with the fresh items.

She was going on her merry way, cleaning and exploring her new kitchen when she realized the relentless noise had stopped. She popped her head around the corner to find Annie asleep on the floor. The poor little mite had worn herself out. It had been a big day for both of them.

She picked Annie up, then carried her into the nursery, placing her carefully in the crib. As she returned to the kitchen she could smell something burning.

"Oh no! Not my soup!" It was all she could do not to cry. This was her first opportunity to impress Jacob with her cooking, and she'd ruined it.

Magdalena quickly added some water, and gave the soup a stir. She stood beside it until it simmered, then added a small amount onto a spoon and tasted it. She breathed a sigh of relief when there was no burned flavor.

While Annie slept, she decided to make biscuits as a surprise for Jacob, and prepared the mixture.

When she was done, Magdalena stood at the window looking out. The sky was darkening. He must surely be coming home soon?

She stoked the stove and added more wood. It was almost time to put the biscuits in the oven. Annie would wake soon, and hopefully Jacob wouldn't be too late. She didn't want him to eat an overcooked meal.

She knew she wasn't the best cook around, but she could get by. She hoped it was enough to keep Jacob satisfied. With her sister working the late shift, Magdalena often prepared meals for William and herself.

She fought back the emotion that threatened to overwhelm her at the thought of her sister and brother-in-law lying dead at the bottom of the Bighorn River. They would never have a burial, and she didn't get to say a proper good-bye.

Tears welled in her eyes and she fought them back.

She stirred the soup again, trying to take her mind off the negative thoughts that had overtaken her, but it didn't work.

At least she hadn't parted from her sister on bad terms. That would have been too much for her to bear. The hardest part was that Annie would never get to know her wonderful parents.

Tears streamed down her face, and she swiped at them. She'd tried hard to fight back her grief since the accident, and now it was overwhelming her.

She sat on the sofa and quietly sobbed.

"Magdalena?" Jacob ran to her. She hadn't even heard him come in. "What's wrong?" He pulled her into his arms, and she felt a little better.

A sob escaped her lips, and she rested her head on his shoulder. His arms went up around her, soothing her with the circles he was rubbing across her back.

She stared at him with tear-filled eyes. "I was thinking about Elizabeth and William, how Annie will never get to know them, and they'll never get to see her grow up, and..."

He put his fingers to her lips, then pulled her closer. "You didn't get a chance to grieve for them," he said gently, and she knew he was right.

"I'm sorry," she said. "I'm bawling like a baby."

He looked around. "Speaking of babies, where is she?"

"Asleep." Magdalena pulled out of his arms. "I have to fix supper." He tried to keep her there. "No, I really have to fix supper or it will burn," she said quietly, wiping at her eyes.

He stood with her, and it was then she noticed the concern on his face. For the first time since she arrived, she thought perhaps there might be a chance they could come to care for each other given time.

Love or anything like it, was far from her thoughts.

Annie was in her highchair, Magdalena sitting close by, feeding her cooled soup.

Jacob looked down at his supper. Despite Magdalena saying she'd ruined it, this soup was by far the best he'd ever had. But he wouldn't tell his sister that.

Over the years he'd had many a meal at Jennifer and Charles' ranch. It was always a circus with the adults trying to eat, and the children running riot.

Finally they'd worked out feeding the children ahead of time would allow the adults to eat in peace. But Magdalena was having none of that.

Annie had always eaten with the family, she'd told him. At least since she'd been able to sit up.

Family. Were they a family?

He supposed they were. But not in the true sense.

A real family was a mother, father, and a bunch of children. *They* were an aunt, a niece, and... truth be known, he had no idea what he was. A husband for sure, but other than that, he honestly didn't know.

He pulled his thoughts back to the delicious food sitting in front of him. The biscuits were good. Very good. Jacob reached for another one and slathered it with butter. He had no idea his new wife was such a good cook. It was certainly a plus as far as he was concerned.

She put another spoonful of soup into the baby's mouth, but she spat it out. "She's had enough," Magdalena said, wiping the mess from Annie's face.

She cleaned up the spilled food around her, then fussed over the child. "Eat your supper," he said between mouthfuls. "It's very good, by the way."

He stared into her face. She seemed to be over her earlier upset, which relieved him. He couldn't imagine losing his sister, let alone his sister and her husband at the same time. Top it off with taking on the responsibility of caring for their children.

He shifted in his seat. He really hadn't been fair to his wife. She may not have understood it until now, but she was definitely in the throes of grief. Perhaps even guilt at having told her sister she was leaving after they returned from their honeymoon.

Ending up dead on the bottom of a river was not his idea of a successful honeymoon.

His head shot up when he heard the child giggling. Her hands were reaching out for a biscuit. "Can she have some?" he asked, not sure if it was alright or not.

"Just a little. She's never had them before."

Annie snatched it up and shoved it in her mouth, slowly sucking on the soft texture. "I think she likes it," he said, and grinned.

Magdalena stared down into her food but made no attempt to eat it. "Are you going to eat that while it's hot?" She was far too skinny already, and couldn't afford to not eat.

She pushed it away. "You can have it if you like."

He frowned. "I have plenty." He scraped his chair back and came next to her, squatting down to her level. "You have to eat," he said, gently touching her shoulder.

She swiveled her head to look at him. "I'm not hungry." The sadness in her eyes hit in right in the heart.

His arm went up around her shoulders. "If you don't eat, I don't eat."

"Oh, that's just silly. I'm not hungry."

He stood abruptly and returned to his place at the table, and sat there, not moving.

"Finish your supper while it's hot," she told him.

She'd obviously not believed what he'd said. He pushed his bowl away from him. "Only if you do," he said, determined. He was not going to be responsible for his wife becoming ill.

"For goodness sakes," she said in a huff, then picked up her spoon and ate slowly.

He waited until she'd almost emptied her bowl before he began to eat again.

He'd already begun to care too much. This wasn't what he'd expected when he sent away for a bride. His idea was for someone to cook and clean, and somewhere down the track, produce an heir for him.

He didn't expect a relationship, and he would have to ensure this didn't go any further than it already had. Magdalena had clearly stated in her letter she needed a husband to support her. There was no mention of anything more.

He reached for another biscuit. "These really are good," he said, wondering what tomorrow night's supper would be.

Chapter Seven

Magdalena lay in bed, her long hair in a plait, her flannelette nightgown keeping her warm.

Jacob was right, it was already getting chilly, and the winter had not yet set in. She'd pulled an extra blanket from the wardrobe, and also added another blanket for Annie.

She wondered when the snow would arrive. Jacob told her it would definitely be there for Christmas, and that was only weeks away.

Her head rested on the soft pillow, and she felt her eyes begin to flutter closed. She knew the exact moment Jacob had climbed into bed as she'd felt the waves of movement ripple across to her side.

Once settled, he reached out and snaked an arm around her waist, pulling her close. She enjoyed his warmth against her back.

"Supper tonight was amazing," he said quietly. "Thank you."

"You're welcome," she answered, wondering why he'd brought it up again. He'd already thanked her at supper, and again when she was washing the dishes.

"I haven't decided yet, but we might have roast tomorrow. If that's what you want, that is."

She felt him shift against her back, and he held her tighter. "Sounds great."

Magdalena knew this was just small talk, leading up to something bigger. But he stayed silent for some minutes and she began to drift off again.

"I'm sorry we got off to such a terrible start," he said, bringing her out of sleep again. His fingers brushed her cheeks, and she couldn't deny she enjoyed when he touched her.

A tingle went down her spine, and warmth spread throughout her body.

He pulled her onto her back, and lifted himself until he was leaning over her, staring into her eyes. He moved slowly toward her, and finally kissed her lips with fiery resolve.

Jacob pulled away, and she wanted him to return. "Do you think we can make it work?" he asked, ignoring the fact he'd just kissed her with a passion he'd never shown before. Worry was etched in his face.

Could they? She hoped so – she'd already come to care for this man, despite his misgivings about her and Annie. Despite his naivety when it came to babies.

She did know Jacob was a good man, a kind man, someone she could come to really care for given time.

She stared up at him, his striking blue eyes piercing her soul, her very being. She licked her lips that were suddenly parched. "I, I hope so," she said softly. "I really do."

His arm slid underneath her, and his head came down again. Magdalena closed her eyes again, but this time knew she wouldn't sleep.

Sunday rolled around quickly, and Magdalena was looking forward to returning to the sweet church where they'd married.

She dressed Annie in her best clothes, put on her thick stockings and warm coat, and placed a pretty bow in her hair. The gloves she'd placed on her hands were already pulled off.

Jacob kept an eye on Annie in the sitting room while Magdalena dressed. She pulled out her favorite dress, but couldn't reach all the fastenings. She was sure Jacob would be happy to help.

He glanced up as she entered the room, a smile on his face. It became bigger when he found out his help was needed.

He pushed her long hair aside, and began to do up the fastenings, his hands sliding over her bare skin. Unnecessarily, in Magdalena's mind.

"Your skin is so soft," he said, leaning in to gently kiss her shoulder.

She sighed. "We need to get ready for church, Jacob." She pivoted her head to look at him. His eyes were full of hunger, of need for her.

Never in her wildest dreams did she believe a man, any man, could have an appetite for her, an old spinster of twenty-eight. She'd always been told she was well past her prime.

He finished the job then spun her in his arms. He stole a kiss before she realized what he was doing. She looked down as she felt a tugging on her gown.

"Oh my gosh, Annie," Magdalena exclaimed. "I'm not sure that is very safe." She watched as Annie tried to pull herself up by grabbing hold of both Magdalena's gown, and Jacob's trouser leg.

As they gazed down at her, she pulled herself into a standing position. Her aunt groaned.

Jacob reached down and picked her up. "She's too small to be doing that, I'm sure," he said. "Jennifer's children crawled first."

So he did know a bit about children after all. "How old were they, can you remember?"

"About this age, I think." He looked thoughtful. "We can ask her at church this morning."

"That would be good. I'll finish dressing and then we can leave." She then left the room, emerging a few minutes later donning her coat and with an elegant hat on her head.

He looked her up and down, his eyes burning into her psyche. Did he do that to every woman he saw, or had he reserved that action only for her?

Magdalena hoped it was for her, and her alone.

Annie was in his arms, clutching her favorite toy, the doll Jacob had bought for her. He pushed the curtain aside and looked out onto the street. "Our cab has arrived."

She pulled on her gloves as they left the house.

The Great Falls church was well attended. Not that Magdalena had expected anything less. They slid into a pew near the back of the church, and sat down, organ music playing in the background. She reached for the bible and held it in her lap, then closed her eyes and prayed for the souls of her sister and brother-in-law.

When she opened them again, she shuddered. Jacob reached across and held her hand. "Are you alright," he asked quietly, concern evident in his voice.

She smiled grimly. "I will be," she said, equally quiet. "I was praying for Elizabeth and William."

He nodded, then squeezed her hands. As the music stopped, Preacher Jones stood out the front, gazing at the congregation and smiling at what he saw.

"Welcome everyone," he said. "It is good to see so many here on such a chilly day. Now let us pray."

Preacher Jones moved to the back of the church as the last hymn was sung. He stood at the entrance and greeted everyone as they left.

"Ah, Mrs Carruthers," he said warmly, as they approached. He reached for her hands and held them gently. "Welcome to our little church. I hope to see you often."

"You will," she said quietly. "This is lovely, but I do miss my church from back home."

Jacob watched as her smile disappeared. He hoped Magdalena would make friends with some of the wonderful ladies from this congregation. He was certain she would fit in well.

"Everyone here is wonderful, friendly," the preacher said, reassuring her, then moved onto the next couple.

They stood outside on the grass, preparing to leave.

"Oh Mr Carruthers," a voice called across to him. "Jacob."

He turned to see Mrs Thompson waving to him, then scurrying toward them. "Oooh, I heard you'd married recently, and wanted to meet your lovely wife. Oh. And your child." She leaned across and reached for Magdalena's hand while gazing at the child. "Hello my dear. Welcome to our little town and our wonderful church."

"This is Mrs Thompson. My wife, Magdalena." He paused for a moment before adding, "This is Magdalena's niece, Annie."

The woman had a huge grin on her face and reached over to touch Annie's cheek, then quickly turned to his wife. "So lovely to meet you, my dear. May I talk to you about the Ladies Auxiliary?" She hooked her arm through Magdalena's and they began to stroll away.

Magdalena glanced back over her shoulder, and pointed to the child. He promised to take care of her.

Everyone moved into the hall where tea and coffee was being prepared. Annie tried to pull out of his arms, but he resisted. Eventually he let her down in a corner of the room, where there was an empty space and she wouldn't be trampled on.

She sat there happily for a while, watching everyone go about their business.

He could see Magdalena in the back of the kitchen with Mrs Thompson and a few of the other ladies from the auxiliary. She seemed in her element.

He'd been holding the doll, and attempted to pass it down to the baby as she was becoming increasingly restless, but she was no longer there. His heart skipped. Where could she have gone so quickly? One moment she was there, and the next she was gone.

He dropped to the floor and glanced around the room, but all he could see were legs and gowns. Panic was beginning to set in. Where was she? And what would Magdalena say when he told her he'd lost her niece?

"Where's Annie?" a scared voice asked.

He got to his feet and gazed at her, guilt wracking him. "I, I don't know. I seemed to have lost her." Her distraught face shocked him. "She was here, and suddenly she wasn't."

She stared at him unbelieving. "She can't walk, Jacob. How could she go, just like that?"

Could someone have taken her? He tensed, then fisted his hands. Surely not...

He didn't wait to explain, but ran around the room, trying to locate the child. He heard Magdalena right behind him, but didn't wait for her.

"Annie?" He looked to the ground, and looked higher as well, since she was now well versed in pulling herself up. "Annie?"

"Annie? Annie?" Magdalena was calling too, the words frantic, her voice high pitched.

Mrs White stepped forward. "Are you looking for this sweetie?" she asked, then stepped aside for them to see. "We didn't know who she belonged to, so couldn't return her."

He pulled Magdalena close, and they watched as Annie crawled along the floor, chasing after the other small children, as though she'd done it a hundred times before.

She was having a great time.

They both breathed a huge sigh of relief. "She's crawling," Magdalena said softly. "She needed a little prompting, I guess."

He tightened his grip on her. "I'm sorry I lost sight of her," Jacob told her, riddled with guilt for the anxiety it caused her.

"You called her Annie."

He gazed at her. "It's her name," he said, puzzled.

"You never call her Annie. You usually call her *the child*." Did he? He frowned. "I'm not complaining," she said. "It's as though you've finally accepted her as part of the family."

There was that word again – *family*. He hadn't thought about it much, but now realized they were a family. He'd never wanted a family, never wanted the responsibility.

But he had to admit to enjoying his new situation, and Annie was an integral part of that.

"Oh, she's crawling!" Jennifer came up behind them, and peeked over Magdalena's shoulder. "How are you settling in?" she asked. "We must get Annie into the children's group," she said without waiting for an answer. "Annie will love spending time with other youngsters."

He knew she was right. You couldn't allow children to be bored. That's when they became destructive.

He thought about his periodicals. Is that what happened? She'd arrived with almost no toys, so what else was there for her to do?

The stroller should arrive soon, but so would the snow, and it would be far too cold for them to go out for long walks. Yes, joining the children's group would be good. It would also help Magdalena get to know some of the other women in town.

Jacob left the two women chatting, and went off to get his wife and sister a coffee. This may turn out for the better.

Chapter Eight

Jacob arrived home from work to a house filled with the aromas of baking. And they were coming from his kitchen, in his house.

He put his briefcase down and hurried to see what Magdalena was making.

He stood in the doorway and breathed in. *Wonderful.*

"What are you making," he asked, then glanced around. The counter was filled with a variety of baked goods.

Magdalena spun around, her hands to her chest. "Oh my gosh, Jacob! You gave me quite a scare."

He stepped forward and took her in his arms. He could feel her heart beating rapidly against him. "I'm sorry," he said, tightening his grip around her.

"I didn't mean to give you a fright. What are you making? It smells superb."

She grinned. "I'm baking for Christmas. It's almost here." She pulled herself out of his grip and picked up three wrapped items. "These three Christmas cakes are those less fortunate than us, and the one in the tin over there is ours."

He couldn't help but feel proud of his wife. He knew she had a good heart, but since she'd joined the Ladies Auxiliary, he'd discovered just how giving she really was.

"I've also made shortbread." She pointed to the ceiling. "And puddings."

He held back a grin. It always amused him the way women hung Christmas puddings from the ceilings. What did it do after all? "You've been busy."

She stared at him. "You don't mind do you? I didn't think you would."

Mind? He adored that she was doing something she loved. The fact she wanted to help others couldn't make him more proud. "Of course not. We have far more than most. It's good to give back to the community."

He could see the relief on her face.

He glanced around. "Where's Annie?" He'd become used to the tot crawling around, and missed her when she wasn't there.

"She's napping. We had children's group today and she thoroughly enjoyed herself. She really loves playing with the other children."

"I'm glad. You both need to spend more time out of the house."

"Supper won't be long. We're having stew tonight, and it's almost ready."

One of his favorites. His life was so much better with his little family in it. How he had managed before, Jacob had no idea.

Jennifer had been right. *A family will be good for you*, she'd said many times, but he hadn't believed her. Now he wouldn't have it any other way.

He loved coming home to the smells of cooking, to a warm house, and a wonderful wife. Not to mention little Annie, who had won his heart. She was like a daughter to him now, and Magdalena was as good as a mother to her.

He was pulled out of his thoughts to the sound of wailing coming from the nursery. When Annie was awake, everyone knew. He smiled at the thought. "I'll get her," he told his wife.

Jacob strolled toward the nursery, knowing full well he'd find her standing in the crib. He wondered how long it would be before she tried to climb out. Hopefully that would be some time off. She was far too small for a regular bed.

As he entered the room, he was greeted with a broad smile. "Pa-pa."

Did she say what he thought she'd said? He swallowed back the lump that had formed in his throat. But he wasn't her papa. Never would be. Not really.

Her little arms reached out to him, and Jacob lifted her from the crib. "You're wet through," he said, holding her away from himself.

He laid her down and changed her diaper. No little surprises, which elicited a sigh of relief. He'd learned how to fold a diaper and apply it correctly. He considered himself a modern man, and unlike most other men in town, was happy to help with what others considered women's work.

As he lifted her again, he was rewarded with a tight hug and a sloppy kiss to his cheek. "Pa-pa," she said again, and his heart warmed.

Was this Annie's way of telling him she'd accepted *him* into *her* family?

"Look who I found," he said, entering the kitchen with Annie in his arms.

"Pa-pa."

Magdalena's eyes opened wide, then tears filled them. "William had been trying to teach her to say that for so long." A tear trickled down her face.

Jacob stepped forward and wiped it away with his thumb. "I feel honored that she sees me that way," he said, the lump in his throat returning. "I love her like a daughter," he said quietly. "I love you both," he said, emotion choking him.

"I love you too, Jacob," Magdalena said equally as quiet. "Even if we did start off on the wrong foot." She looked up into his face, and touched his cheek. It sent a shiver through him. "I know it was difficult in the beginning, but things have worked out for the best."

He pulled her close, and they hugged each other, and Annie. His wonderful family meant the world to him.

"The house looks amazing, Jennifer!"

Jacob watched as Magdalena glanced excitedly around the room with all its Christmas decorations. A small tree stood in the corner with gifts under it, and the children hovered around, waiting to open presents.

Charles looked sternly at them and they quickly dispersed. Magdalena held back a grin, but Jacob could see through her. Their eyes met, and he knew immediately what she was thinking – how could you not laugh?

They'd arrived with a box of baked goodies as their contribution to the celebrations. Jennifer looked inside the box, then breathed deeply. "Oh my gosh, they smell amazing!" She took the box and placed it in the kitchen.

"Thank you," Magdalena said meekly. He'd noticed she was not one to boast about her talents, which he found very humbling.

"Jacob, why don't you show Maggie around? I'll keep an eye on Annie. I'm sure she'll enjoy playing with the children."

He placed gifts around the tree for his nieces and nephews, then took Magdalena on a tour of the property. He showed her around the house first, and then they donned their coats and went outside.

"There's not a lot to see," he said, his arm around her waist. "This is the chicken house, and over there is the barn." He led her toward a paddock where the horses ran free, but she kept her distance from the fence line.

"You don't like horses?" he asked, surprised.

"I, I've never seen one before."

He was surprised, but shouldn't be. She had lived in the city, after all.

He took her hand and led her closer to the fence, then gently held her hand and stretched it out toward the horses. Ginger, the most placid of the two came forward. He sniffed her hand but turned away when she had nothing to offer.

She snatched her hand back.

"Don't be so quick," Jacob told her, then reached into his pocket. Ginger immediately turned back, sensing a reward close by.

He held out a piece of carrot, which was quickly snatched up. "Your turn." He held her hand again, and put a piece of carrot on it. "He won't hurt you."

He spoke gently to the horse, who came over and snatched up the offering as though he was stealing it. Magdalena squealed in fright.

Ginger backed off, then stared at Magdalena, looking her up and down. "It's okay, boy," Jacob told the horse gently, then pulled out another piece of carrot. "Honestly, he won't hurt you. Ready to try again?"

Magdalena hesitated, but put out her hand, ready to take the carrot. As though he understood, Ginger slowly moved toward her, then leaned down and gently took the piece of carrot balanced on her hand.

He stood nearby, chewing on the treat. Jacob watched in delight as the horse moved in and gently nudged Magdalena's shoulder, and whinnied into her neck.

"He likes you," Jacob said, absolutely delighted. "There's lots more to see," he said, leading her further down the property.

"Annie will love this when she's older," his wife said, and he was sure it was true. Jacob led her to the edge of a small forest. "This is where Charles found their Christmas tree. I thought perhaps we might find one too?"

She stared at him. "Perhaps next year? Annie might pull it over the way she is now – pulling herself up on everything."

He hadn't thought of that. "Ah yes. Of course." They began to walk in the opposite direction. "Charles has cattle, and also has a market garden. The farm is self-sufficient as well as selling their produce."

"It's wonderful." Magdalena breathed in the fresh air. "It's so pretty here as well."

They were about to turn back when it began to snow. She put her hands out to catch it. "You did tell me it would snow for Christmas," she said, absolutely delighted.

"We should head back. It could get quite heavy and we don't want to be stuck out here." He pulled her close and held her tight. "This is the best Christmas I've ever had. I'm so grateful to have my own family for Christmas."

He watched as her chin quivered and she held tears back. He was feeling as emotional as she seemed to be.

When they finally arrived back at the cabin, the fire was roaring, and the children were sitting around singing Christmas carols. Annie was in the midst of them, Jennifer by her side.

Jacob pulled his wife a little closer, and she snuggled further into him. "This is the best Christmas ever," he whispered in her ear.

He felt a shiver go through her. "It certainly is," she said. "I never imagined I'd have a family for Christmas."

The children sat around the table wide-eyed. Magdalena was impressed with their behavior. Not one of them misbehaved, and they all ate what was dished out onto their plates.

She could see the children were all happy, but they had obviously been warned to behave. She liked it.

Once luncheon was over, everyone huddled around the tree. Jacob handed out the gifts they'd bought for his nieces and nephews, and Jennifer gave Annie a gift. She was more interested in the wrapping than the toy itself, until she opened it and cuddled the teddy bear she'd been gifted.

Jacob turned to his wife. "I have something for you, too," he said, staring into her eyes.

"I thought we agreed not to buy each other gifts," she protested.

He put his fingers to her lips. "This is different."

How could it be different? A gift is a gift. He pulled a thick envelope out of his pocket. "I've been making enquiries," he said quietly, so the children wouldn't hear. "You know I consider Annie as my own daughter."

She certainly did. He treated her as though she was of his own blood.

He handed her the envelope. "Open it."

She hesitated, then opened it up. Jennifer looked on expectantly.

Tears came to her eyes, then she reached over and hugged her husband with all her might.

"What is it," Jennifer demanded.

She couldn't answer, she was too choked with emotion, so Jacob answered for her. "It's the paperwork for us both to legally adopt Annie," he said, his voice wavering. "That is if Magdalena wants to do it."

"Of course I do," she answered, ending on a sob. "This is the best Christmas gift I've ever received."

Seconds later Annie crawled over and pulled herself up to Jacob. "Pa-pa."

Magdalena couldn't stop her tears from flowing.

Epilogue

Twelve months later...

The screams coming from his wife were heart-wrenching.

Doc Franklin and his nurse had been brilliant. Jennifer was there too, and had ordered him to leave and take Annie with him.

In some ways he was relieved – Jacob couldn't take it any more. Besides, Annie shouldn't be hearing that. What must she think was happening to her mother?

Why did childbirth have to be so cruel?

He bundled Annie up in warm clothes and covered her with a blanket, then placed her in the stroller.

He had no idea where they were going, but headed toward town, despite the flurries around them.

Before long, he found himself in the Mercantile.

"Morning Jacob." Cecil greeted him warmly.

"Oh, yes. Good morning."

"You seem a little distracted today. Is everything alright?" He looked down into the stroller. "Good morning Miss Annie."

Annie lifted a glove-covered hand and waved, grinning at the same time. "Hello Mider Del," she said, still unable to pronounce his name correctly. It was difficult after all.

"Magdalena is in childbirth," he said, feeling more worried as the time ticked by. "We were ordered out."

Cecil frowned. "I'm sure they'll both be fine," he said. "I'll pray for them."

Jacob knew he would and nodded his thanks.

"What say we find a new toy for you, Annie?" her father asked.

He was rewarded with little hands clapping and the biggest grin he'd ever seen. They worked their way to where the toys were kept, and he picked her up so Annie could study the selection.

She pointed at a stuffed lamb. It was pure white, soft and cuddly and had a huge red bow around its neck. "Dis one, Papa," Annie said, her eyes sparkling.

Jacob handed it to her. She snuggled into it, and he knew she'd made the right choice.

They returned to the counter, and Cecil added it to his account. "I hope everything goes well," he said as they were about to leave.

Jennifer stormed through the door. "You need to come back, Jacob."

He stared at her. "Is everything alright?"

"Look at my new toy." Annie held the toy in the air to show her aunt.

"It's beautiful, sweetie," she said, then turned to Jacob. "The baby has arrived," she said, grinning this time. "Come on, hurry up!" Then scurried off again before he could ask if it was a boy or girl.

Jacob looked lovingly down at his new daughter, Elsa Rose, Annie standing nearby. "Baby," she said, gently touching the baby's cheek.

He'd been excited and hesitant all at the same time when Magdalena had told him the news.

With Annie, their legally adopted daughter, being so young herself, he knew it would be a handful for his wife.

She refused his offer of a nanny, as he knew she would. She wanted to bring up their daughters herself. Neither of them wanted to miss a moment of their young lives.

Suddenly Annie turned tail and ran into her bedroom, returning with the doll and teddy bear she loved so much. He'd spoiled her with many toys since she'd arrived, but those were still her favorites.

He was touched when she tried to give them to the baby.

Jennifer stood over him as he sat on the edge of the bed. "She's beautiful," she said, her voice wavering despite having been there when Elsa was born.

"Yes, she is," Magdalena said, still recovering from giving birth. She turned to Jacob. "Don't think this is going to become a habit," she said forcefully.

He grinned then sobered. "I have been given such a precious gift two Christmases in a row," he said, then leaned in and kissed her gently on the lips. "I love you so much."

Jacob reached down and pulled Annie up onto his lap, and hugged her tight. A little over a year ago, he had no idea he would have a family for Christmas.

He didn't know what the coming years would bring, but he knew no matter what happened, their family would be full of love for each other.

THE END

From the Author

Thank you so much for reading my book – I hope you enjoyed it.

I would greatly appreciate you leaving a review on Amazon, even if it is only a one-liner. It helps to have my books more visible on Amazon!

All my books can be seen on my Amazon Author Page - https://www.amazon.com/Cheryl-Wright/e/B0088GDSKM/.

You might also enjoy reading other books in the Spinster Mail-Order Brides:

Bonus Book – A Shadowed Groom for Christmas – Marisa Masterson -

https://www.amazon.com/gp/product/B07SNFSW38

Book 1 - A Marshal for Christmas - P. Creeden
https://www.amazon.com/dp/B07TRBKRYS

Book 2 – A Bride for Christmas – Cheryl Wright
https://www.amazon.com/dp/B07SJXTFPY

Book 3 - A Husband for Christmas - Margaret Tanner
https://www.amazon.com/Husband-Christmas-Spinster-Order-Brides-ebook/dp/B07SSP47BN/

Book 4 - A Farmer for Christmas- Marisa Masterson
https://www.amazon.com/dp/B07T2MY829